A Thanksgiving of Surprises

ISBN 978-1-64349-511-8 (paperback)
ISBN 978-1-64349-512-5 (digital)

Christian Faith Publishing, Inc.
832 Park Avenue
Meadville, PA 16335
www.christianfaithpublishing.com

Printed in the United States of America

A Thanksgiving of Surprises

Barbara Pappal

Emily could smell cooked oatmeal as she stepped inside the door of their white farmhouse on a drizzly Thanksgiving Day.

"Good morning, Emily," her mom said as she handed Emily a cup of hot chocolate. "Are you done feeding Blaze?"

"Yes, Mom," said Emily sitting down at the table eating her bowl of oatmeal sprinkled with brown sugar, "Blaze is eating his healthy breakfast of grains too."

Blaze was a young horse given to Emily when she was four, and she had learned to ride him with her dad's assistance during equestrian training. Blaze and Emily became pals, spending time galloping over the farm land.

Mom reminded Emily of the day's plan, spending Thanksgiving with her grandparents. Emily and her sister Ann were excited because Grandma always had holiday surprises.

Grandma had taught Emily this day was a celebration of giving thanks to the Lord Jesus, established by President Lincoln, but our first President George Washington also declared a day of Thanksgiving to honor the Supreme Being, God, who blessed our new nation. The Pilgrims celebrated a three-day feast in thanks for their survival, bountiful harvest, and the land God had guided the Mayflower to Plymouth Rock. Emily also learned how the Indians helped the Pilgrims to grow corn and use herbs for medicine. It was always fun to see what Grandma would teach each year about Thanksgiving.

Emily was about to shower for the day's visit when her dad came inside and said the heifers had gotten out of an unlocked fence gate and were in the small orchard nearby. This certainly was an unexpected surprise event.

Emily asked, "May Blaze and I help?"

"Sure, Emily," her dad said.

Emily went to the barn and could tell Blaze was surprised to see her again so soon. He neighed as her dad helped with the saddle and Emily mounted him. It didn't take long to round up and lead the heifers through the gate with Emily's Dad on his horse too. It was fun, and soon Emily was taking Blaze back to his clean stall. Emily hugged and kissed Blaze good-bye. Blaze neighed again.

After a fresh shower, she changed into a fluffy pink blouse and blue skinny jeans and arranged her curly red hair with just a couple swoops of the brush.

During the short drive to Emily's grandparents' town house, Emily and her younger sister, Ann, sang pop songs together in the car. The sunlight began to ray through the clouds as the rain diminished. Suddenly, a beautiful double rainbow appeared. Another big and pleasant surprise!

When they arrived, Grandma greeted everyone at the door and said, "Hi, everybody, I have a surprise for you! I'm serving roasted duck!"

Immediately Emily became doubtful of liking this surprise in place of the traditional meal.

Ann whispered in her ear, "Have you ever tasted duck?"

"No," said Emily, "and I don't think I want to. But let's be nice to Grandma."

Grandma began explaining the traditional Thanksgiving meal has changed from the original Thanksgiving celebration of the Pilgrims and Indians. She chose to serve roast duck as an additional choice the Pilgrims had.

"The Pilgrims would have eaten venison and other water fowl," said Grandma. "And they didn't have potatoes but ate corn, but we will have the mashed potatoes."

The whole family loved Grandma's buttery, fluffy mashed potatoes, and Grandma knew it.

Grandma pulled the browned orange flavored duck from the oven, carved it, and placed it on the buffet. Tiny beads of oil lie on the sliced fowl.

Suddenly Emily's grandpa rang the dinner bell. Everyone sat around the oak table covered with fine white linen and china. Dad said grace and thanked God for his blessings. Grandma asked everyone to thank God of a special blessing. Emily thanked the Lord for Blaze. Ann was thankful for the rainbows.

Emily tasted the roasted duck first and spoke unexpectedly, "Oh, it is sweet, orange and oily tasting, much different than turkey!"

Emily tried not to show her disappointment. Grandma smiled. And then another surprise! The platter of turkey and stuffing was being passed also. What a relief! Grandma winked, and Emily giggled. Emily never noticed that the turkey had been sitting in the top oven already carved with its trimmings. Grandma was always thoughtful and never disappointed. She understood and was very pleased that Emily introduced herself to the taste of roasted duck.

Grandma served pumpkin pie covered with walnuts and whipped cream later in the afternoon. She told Emily and her sister that the Pilgrims no doubt had nuts, pumpkins, and other fruits such as wild grapes to eat, and possibly baked pie, but she didn't know if they had already built stone ovens. Emily took another small serving of the fresh cranberry Jell-O™ salad with pineapple.

"Oh yes," said Grandma. "The Pilgrims no doubt ate fresh cranberries too."

It had been a fun experience, talking about the menu of the First Thanksgiving.

Pilgrims' Thanksgiving Menu

Wildfowl/Venison/Seafood
Corn/peas/onions/Beans
Wild Berries/Cranberries
Grapes
Acorns/Nuts
Bread
Pumpkin
Water

A Modern Thanksgiving Menu

Turkey
Stuffing
Potatoes/Candied Yams
Vegetables
Cranberry Salad
Lettuce Salad
Dinner Rolls
Pumpkin Pie and Various Baked Goods
Beverage

21

The day passed away quickly with fun and board games. Grandma liked old traditions and didn't play any computer games. Grandpa was the best at Monopoly™ and would let Emily win sometimes.

Later, Emily's mom spoke softly to Emily, "I'm happy the way you dealt with all of your surprises today."

Then Emily said, "Surprise!" She leaned forward to blow kisses to her mom and dad, and spoke again, "I'm thankful for such a wonderful family, and I will always have a special memory of this Thanksgiving Day."

As the car drove up the lane to their farmhouse, Emily saw Blaze looking out the barn window and yelled out, "I love you, Blaze."

And he neighed.

About the Author

The author, Barbara Pappal, has been a Christian since a teenager and is a retired secretary. She has been married for forty-seven years to her husband, Charles Jr., and has enjoyed her faith in the Lord with him many years. She has a son, a daughter, a daughter-in-law, a son-in-law, three grandchildren and two step-grandchildren. Barbara enjoys reading to her grandchildren and dedicates this book to them.

This children's book was inspired by her childhood, growing up on a dairy farm.

CPSIA information can be obtained
at www.ICGtesting.com
Printed in the USA
LVHW072131270619
622612LV00023B/1046/P